THE PARABLE OF
THE LOST SHEEP

Jesus told this parable.

"*Suppose one of you has a hundred sheep and loses one of them—what does he do? He leaves the other ninety nine sheep in the pasture and goes looking for the one that got lost, until he finds it. When he finds it, he is so happy that he puts it on his shoulders and carries it back home. Then he calls his friends and neighbours together and says to them, 'I am so happy I found my lost sheep. Let us celebrate!' In the same way, I tell you, there will be more joy in heaven over one sinner who repents than over ninety nine respectable people who do not need to repent.*"

St Luke 15, 4-7

Acknowledgment

The above quotation from The Good News Bible *is reproduced by permission of The British and Foreign Bible Society and Collins Publishers.*

The parable of
THE
LOST SHEEP

retold for easy reading
by SYLVIA MANDEVILLE

illustrated by DAVID PALMER

Ladybird Books Loughborough

THE LOST SHEEP

It was early morning, and Daniel the shepherd was counting his sheep. They had been sleeping all night in the sheep pen, safe from danger.

"One, two, three, four," he counted as they scampered

past. "Fifteen, sixteen, seven-teen." The sheep bleated and butted into each other. "Twenty five, twenty six," Daniel counted carefully. "Forty one, forty two ... sixty four, sixty five." Until at last there were only three sheep left in the pen.

"Ninety eight, ninety nine, a hundred!" said Daniel. "Now we can start the day."

He loved his sheep and although he had so many, he knew them all by name.

"Spotty! Black Ear! Big Patch!" he called. Three of the biggest sheep looked up when they heard his voice, and began to follow him. Then the rest moved after him too.

The sheep were hungry now and were ready for Daniel to lead them through the hills to the fresh grass.

Daniel was always ready too for this early morning walk. He was stiff and aching, because all night long he had been curled up asleep in the gap in the wall of the sheep pen. There was no proper door in the wall. Daniel had to be the door, and no one could get through into the sheep pen without waking him.

It was a lonely life being a shepherd, but Daniel loved it. He loved the quietness of the hills, the cold starry nights, and the gentle bleating of his sheep. He was in full charge of them and had to keep them safe by day and by night.

The way led through a dark narrow gorge. Tall rocks towered high overhead on either side. The sheep did not like this shadowy part of the journey. The darkness frightened them.

To let the sheep at the back of the flock know that he was still leading them, Daniel banged on the overhanging rocks with his stick. The sheep heard his knocks echoing back to them in the gloom. Then they knew that he was still there in front of them, and they felt safe.

Suddenly they were out in the bright sunshine on the other side. The lush green grass smelt warm and sweet. The brook glinted and sparkled. Here the sheep would be content.

Daniel filled his bottle with cool water from the stream and took it back with him to the shade of a tree. Then he unwrapped some bread from his bag.

This was the best part of the day. It was still cool and the sheep were busy eating. For a moment, Daniel lay back in the grass and looked up into the cloudless sky.

"How wonderful the world is that God has made," he thought, then he rolled over onto his stomach and lay there, eating his bread and watching the sheep.

During the whole of the day he had to be on guard. It was no good sleeping during the day while his sheep were out in the open. There was too much danger.

He thought of the time when a bear had come ambling up, hoping for a lamb. He remembered the watchful eagles always on the look out for a sick animal to snatch.

As he lay watching, he noticed that Big Patch was wandering off on his own, looking for better grass in the distance. Soon he would be out of sight.

Daniel sat up. He picked up his sling and a smooth pebble. Carefully he took aim.

Plop! The pebble landed on a rock just in front of Big Patch. It did not touch him, but the noise frightened him, and he ran quickly back to join the other sheep.

As the sun rose high in the sky and it got hotter and hotter, Daniel took out his small harp to play. His sheep loved hearing him sing and play – songs about sheep and farms, songs about fights with wild animals, and songs about God's care.

All the time he was singing, he was searching the rocks and undergrowth for any signs of danger.

Suddenly, Daniel flung the harp to the ground. He seized a stick and ran shouting over the grass. He picked up a rock as he ran and hurled it.

He had seen a lion creeping silently over the rocks. He was not going to let it eat one of his sheep!

The noise of Daniel's foot-steps, his loud cries, and the crash of the rock frightened the lion. The flock of sheep ran off amongst the rocks, and the lion saw no chance of snatching one. It bounded off with a roar.

Quickly Daniel ran back to his sheep. He called them all by name and gathered them together. He counted them to make sure that they were all there, and then he talked to them.

The sight of the lion had made them tremble, and his kind voice calmed them.

Daniel knew a shady place
among the rocks where they
would feel safe, and he led
them there now. The rest of
the day passed quietly.

Then as evening drew near, Daniel led his sheep for the last time that day, up the path to the top of the hill to the sheep pen. Daniel always looked forward to that part of the day.

After he had counted his sheep and got them safely in the pen, he would light a fire and sit by it and eat his supper.

Far below him he would watch the lights in the houses in the little town. Far above him he would count the stars.

Then when it was late, he would curl up in the gateway and sleep himself. Tonight, he had some special supper and he was looking forward to it.

But first he must count his sheep.

"One, two, three, four...
thirty, thirty one, thirty two..."
Sometimes two pushed through
together, but he never got
muddled. "Eighty eight, eighty

nine…" There went Spotty and Black Ear. "Ninety nine…"

Daniel looked round for Big Patch. He was nowhere to be seen.

"Big Patch! Big Patch!" Daniel called, but there was no answer. To make sure, Daniel went into the pen and counted the flock again.

No, there were only ninety nine there, and Daniel was sure that it was Big Patch who was missing.

What should he do? Big Patch had to be found, but how could he leave the other sheep alone?

Daniel thought of the lion and of all the other dangers of the night. He would have to leave the other ninety nine sheep on their own. There was nothing else he could do.

Calling out "Big Patch!" in a loud voice, he strode off down the path. It was getting difficult to see now, for it was nearly dark. Many times he tripped over the rocks. Thorns and brambles scratched him.

"Where else can he be?" Daniel wondered. "Where can he have wandered to?"

Daniel knew that however long it took, he must go on searching until he found Big Patch. He thought of the rocky place they had stayed at that day, and made his way there.

"Big Patch! Big Patch!" he called. Suddenly through the darkness, Daniel heard a bleat. It was not very loud. It was not very strong, but it *was* a bleat, and Daniel could tell it was Big Patch.

"I'm coming!" he called, and again he heard the feeble cry. "He must be stuck somewhere in between some rocks," said Daniel. He called again and listened very carefully for the answer.

It was coming from down below him. Big Patch had fallen over the edge of a cliff, onto a ledge, and could not get back up.

Calling to Big Patch and talking to him all the time to calm him, Daniel slowly climbed down the cliff ledge. The rocks had broken and slipped and there was little room for his feet. Daniel saw that Big Patch would soon have fallen down the cliff to the bottom.

As Daniel reached the ledge, Big Patch gave a bleat. He was glad to see his good shepherd.

Daniel grabbed Big Patch and hugged him tight. When he had calmed him down, he lifted him up onto his shoulders and carefully climbed back up the cliff onto the path.

All the way back to his flock, Daniel sang happily. "I've got my Big Patch here, safe and sound," he said. "He could have been lost for ever, but I found him. I shall have a party. I shall invite the other shepherds. I shall send a young boy down to the village with a message, and invite my family and neighbours.

"I shall say, 'Come and have a good time. Be happy with me, because I have found my lost sheep.'"

Even though it was now quite dark and the way was uphill, Daniel soon reached his flock again.

He was so excited. He got out some oil and rubbed it onto the scratches on Big Patch's legs. He checked him for other wounds, and pulled thorns and brambles from his wool. Then he let Big Patch run to join the rest of the flock.

Quickly Daniel lit the fire and ate his supper. He was too excited to sleep. He looked up at the great buttercup field of stars.

"What a day!" he said. "First the lion, then finding Big Patch – and tomorrow a party. I'm so glad I found him."

Jesus says that God our Father loves us like a shepherd. God is happier when one person says sorry and turns to love Him, than when ninety nine other people have no need of His forgiveness.